This book belongs to:

_____

_____

_____

First published 2005 by Walker Books Ltd
87 Vauxhall Walk, London SE11 5HJ

This edition published 2012

2 4 6 8 10 9 7 5 3 1

© 1990 – 2012 Lucy Cousins
Lucy Cousins font © 1990 – 2012 Lucy Cousins

Illustrated in the style of Lucy Cousins by King Rollo Films Ltd.

Maisy™. Maisy is a trademark of Walker Books Ltd, London.

The right of Lucy Cousins to be identified as author/illustrator of this
work has been asserted by her in accordance with the Copyright,
Designs and Patents Act 1988.

Printed in China

British Library Cataloguing in Publication Data:
a catalogue record for this book is available from the British Library.

ISBN 978-1-4063-4458-5

www.walker.co.uk

Maisy Goes
to the Library

Lucy Cousins

WALKER BOOKS
AND SUBSIDIARIES

LONDON · BOSTON · SYDNEY · AUCKLAND

Maisy likes going to the library.

How lovely to look at a book in a nice quiet place.

It was the sort of day when Maisy wanted a book about fish.

She found a flappy book about birds ... but no fish.

She found a shiny green book about turtles ...

and a great big stripy
book about tigers...
but no fish!

Never mind,
there are
so many
other things
to do in
the library...

make a copy of your favourite picture...

look at the fish in the aquarium...

Aquarium?

That's it! So Maisy looked
by the aquarium...

and that's exactly where
she found a book about fish...
and it was sparkly!

Maisy settled down
to read in a quiet corner.

But then Cyril and Tallulah came along...

and started laughing (at Tallulah's funny face!).

And then Eddie came in ...

because Ostrich was going to tell a story in the Story corner...

Maisy's quiet corner!

"There was an old woman, who swallowed a fly..."

Charley started laughing.

"She swallowed a dog to catch the cat!"

Then everyone started laughing!

And they were still laughing when they checked out their books,

and went outside
to play.

In the park, Cyril and Charley pretended to be the old woman and her dog.

Woof-woof!

Tallulah meowed like a cat ... and Eddie neighed like a horse.

Meeow! And Maisy...?

Neigh!

Maisy read
her sparkly book
about fish in a
nice ... *quiet* ...
place...

My friend Maisy

ISBN 978-1-4063-7404-9

ISBN 978-1-4063-7152-9

ISBN 978-1-4063-9768-0

ISBN 978-1-4063-9760-4

It's more fun with Maisy!

Available from all good booksellers

www.maisyfun.com